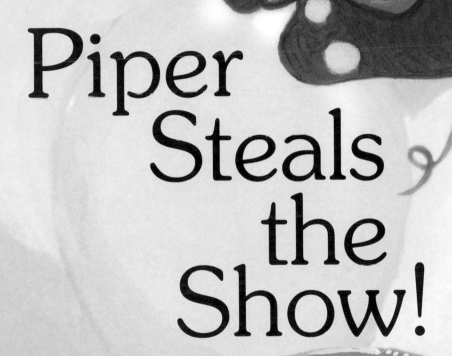

Piper
Steals
the
Show!

by
Mark Lowry and
Martha Bolton

Illustrated by Kristen Myers

HOWARD
PUBLISHING CO.

Our purpose at Howard Publishing is to:

- *Increase faith* in the hearts of growing Christians
- *Inspire holiness* in the lives of believers
- *Instill hope* in the hearts of struggling people everywhere

Because He's coming again!

Piper Steals the Show!
©2000 Mark Lowry
All rights reserved. Printed in the United States of America

Published by Howard Publishing Co., Inc.,
3117 North 7th Street, West Monroe, Louisiana 71291-2227

00 01 02 03 04 05 06 07 08 09   10 9 8 7 6 5 4 3 2 1

Illustrated by Kristen Myers
Digital Enhancement by Vanessa Bearden

Library of Congress Cataloging-in-Publication Data
Lowry, Mark.
    Piper steals the show / Mark Lowry

    ISBN 1-58229-127-6

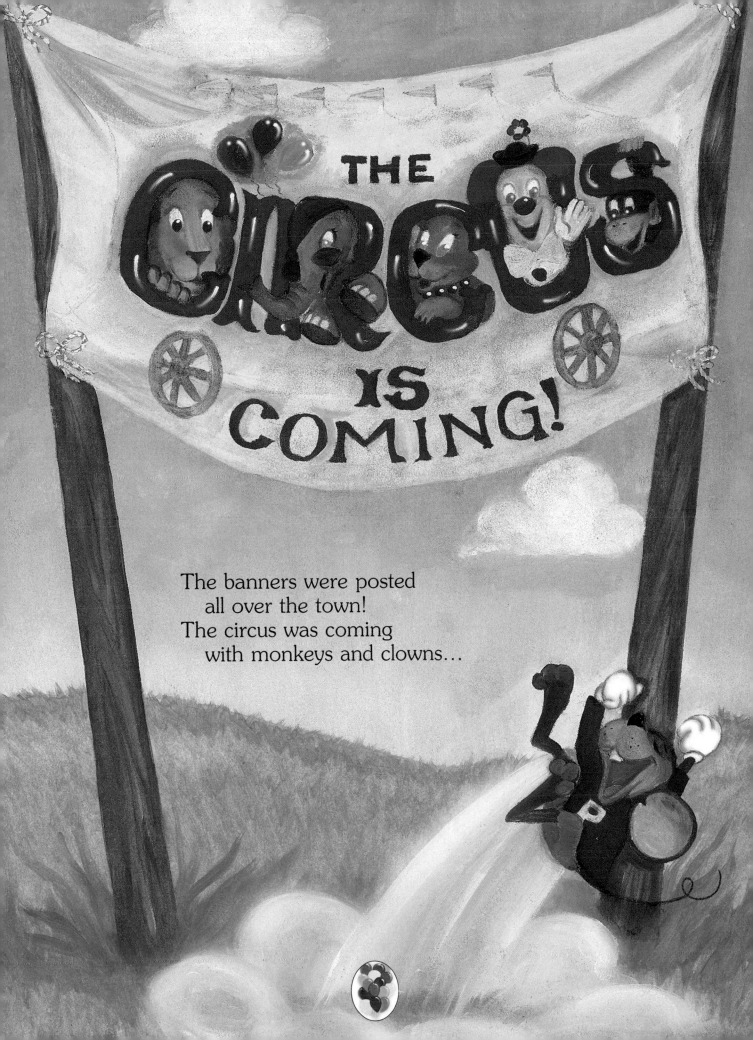

THE CIRCUS IS COMING!

The banners were posted
all over the town!
The circus was coming
with monkeys and clowns...

And tigers and lions
    and elephants, too!
Piper heard the train whistle,
    and he knew just what to do.

"Can we go? Can we go?
    Can we go?" Piper said.
"Can we go?" He repeated,
    but his mom shook her head.

"Son, I'm so sorry,
   but there's just no way.
The circus costs more
   than a field mouse can pay."

"Then, may I go
   and just look at the tent?"
His mom said, "OK,"
   and so off Piper went.

Racing down Swiss Lane
and up Gouda Street.
He was moving just like
there were jets on his feet!

He rounded a corner...

And slid to a stop,
   for there right before him
   was the circus big top!

He tried to resist,
but the pull was too great.
And he wondered who'd see him
if he slipped through the gate.

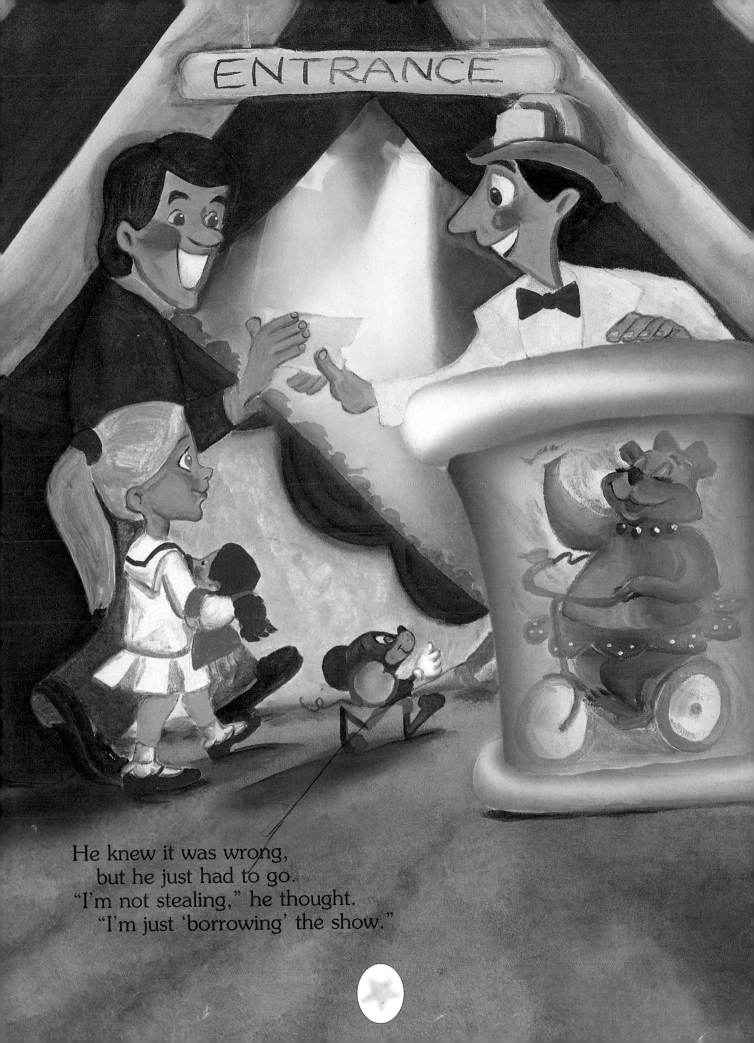

He knew it was wrong,
   but he just had to go.
"I'm not stealing," he thought.
   "I'm just 'borrowing' the show."

The bleachers were filled,

so he wandered backstage...

And found a red stool
  by the lion's big cage.
"I'll just borrow this stool
  till the circus is through,
And I'll borrow these stilts
  and the bear's tu tu, too."

BACKSTAGE

The things Piper borrowed?
  Well, who could keep track?
He was turning into
  a kleptomousiac!

Piper snickered and said,
  "It won't hurt anyone.
I'll put it all back
  when I'm done with my fun!"

So he put on the tu tu
  and climbed on the stool,
Then danced on the stilts.
  He was feeling soooo cool!

So he leaped from the stilts,
landing right on a tray.

Through a big cloud of pink,
he heard people screaming,
"There's a mouse on that tray!"
How he wished he was dreaming!

There was no place to hide,
    for the bear was now on.
She was bare and quite mad,
    for her tu tu was gone!

Her gaze met with Piper's,
    and off that bear went,
Chasing Piper the Mouse
    through the whole circus tent!

It was time for the lions
to enter the ring.
"Where's my stool?!"
yelled the tamer.
"Who's been stealing
our things?!"

While he ranted and raved
'bout the nerve of the louse,
The bear and the lions were
chasing that mouse!

The clown entered next,
did a bit of a dance,

But without his big stilts,
he just tripped on his pants!

He joined in the chase,
but he didn't get far.
It's hard to go fast
in a little clown car.

The ringmaster tried
   to regain some control,
But that hyper mouse
   had just stolen the show!

Piper ran for the exit.
    He tried to look back,
But he should've looked straight
    'cause he headed right SMACK...

Into the leg of a
    six-year-old kid
Who'd been crying because
    of what someone did.

"I was holding two tickets
for my dad and for me,
When someone just took them.
They stole them, you see?"

Piper couldn't believe it!
He was shocked!
He was mad that someone would
steal from this kid and his dad!

Then Piper remembered
the things he had done,
And all of his "borrowing"
was no longer fun.

Yes, Piper was learning a
lesson that day.
When you take what's not yours,
someone still has to pay.

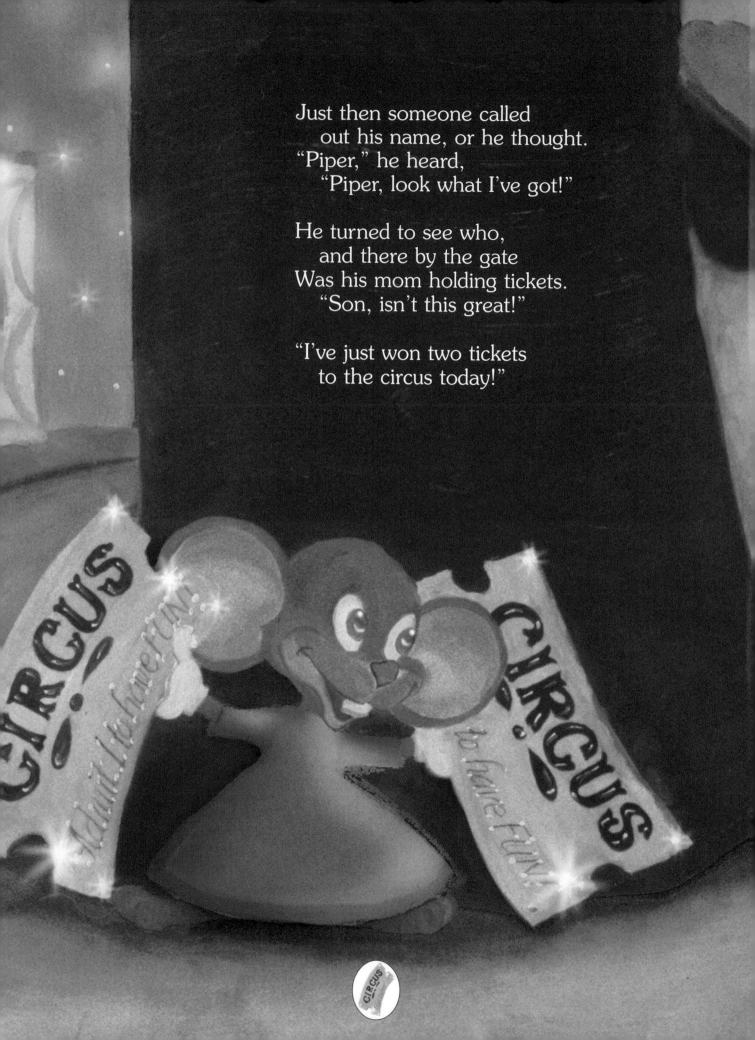

Just then someone called
    out his name, or he thought.
"Piper," he heard,
    "Piper, look what I've got!"

He turned to see who,
    and there by the gate
Was his mom holding tickets.
    "Son, isn't this great!"

"I've just won two tickets
    to the circus today!"

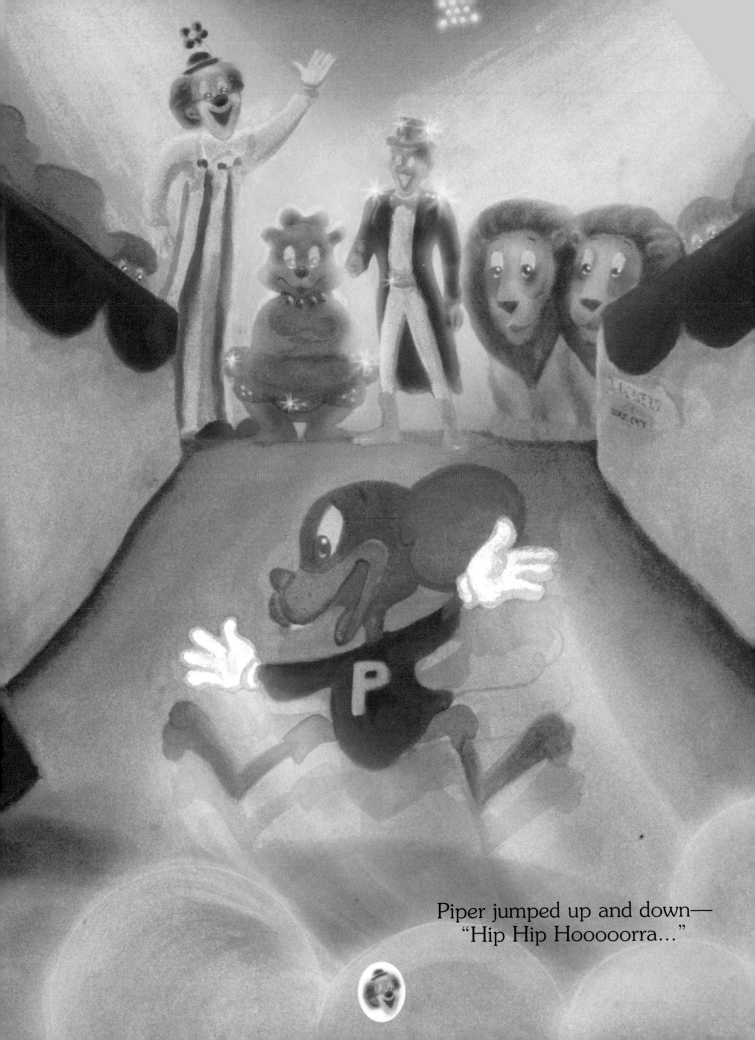

Piper jumped up and down—
"Hip Hip Hooooorra…"

Love your neighbor as yourself

But Piper couldn't get that boy from his mind.
And he knew God would want him to do something kind.

So he asked Mom's permission. She nodded, and then...

CIRCUS
Admit 1 to have FUN!

Piper gave up his tickets
so they could get in.

The ringmaster praised him!
The audience cheered!
And his mother was beaming
mouse ear to mouse ear!

The clown on his stilts
carried Piper around.
The mayor even named him
"The Mouse of the Town!"

Piper danced with the bear,
who now had her tu tu,
And rode on the lions,
and when he was through…

They asked him to speak.
  Piper said, "Now I know
That this is the way
  a mouse should steal the show!"